Forgiveness

Teamwork

Prudence

Social Intelligence

Spirituality

Self Regulation

Fairness

Curiosity

Appreciation
of Beauty & Excellence

Leadership

Creativity

Gratitude

Hope

Humour

Zest

Honesty

Bravery

Perspective

Love of Learning

Love

Perseverance

Kindness

Humility

Open Minded

Dear Sean, Connor, Isabella, and Kyan.

You inspire me every day with your boundless curiosity,
patience, love and support.
This is for you, my shining stars, who light up my world with
joy and possibility. May you always believe in the power of
your dreams and the strength within you to make them
come true.

Being and Belonging

Written by Tenille Dowe
Illustrated by Tenille Dowe

First Printing, 2024
Published by Creative Heart Connection

 Creative Heart Connection

 creative.heart.connection

ISBN 9781763592858

Being and Belonging

Character Strengths Edition

Written and Illustrated
by Tenille Dowe

Her dreams brought to life.
Feeling gratitude for her precious gift.
Curiosity overflowing for the life within.
A mother's journey about to begin.

The fragile shell suddenly
softens and cracks,
revealing multiple arms and legs!
Too many for just one egg.

Like clowns overflowing from a tiny car.
New lives!
Not able to contain their humour, laughter and cheer.
Loud, cheeky giggles for all to hear.

Each born a reflection of the other.
A love of learning from one another.

Soaking in the world around,
knowledge flowing from their head to the ground.

Her heart filled with hope,
for all lessons she could impart.

The other, leadership was her
goal from the start.

Not knowing much at all,
but standing tall, not wanting to fall.

Not knowing which way to run,
with prudence as her compass her journey
had begun.

She approached life's challenges with a
combination of caution and courage.
Eating it all up like a bowl full of warm
porridge.

Always weighing the risks and rewards.

Learning to harness her anxious energy,
ensuring that every step forward was taken
with calculated precision at her core.

Emotions build up,
waiting for the moment
to pounce.

Awareness and self regulation
must not be blocked,
when all fear can do is,
knock, knock, knock.

Fear and anxiety on high alert,
just doing her best to get by.
Her feelings and emotions
inside and unseen.
Emotions drained life.
She is now white, not green.

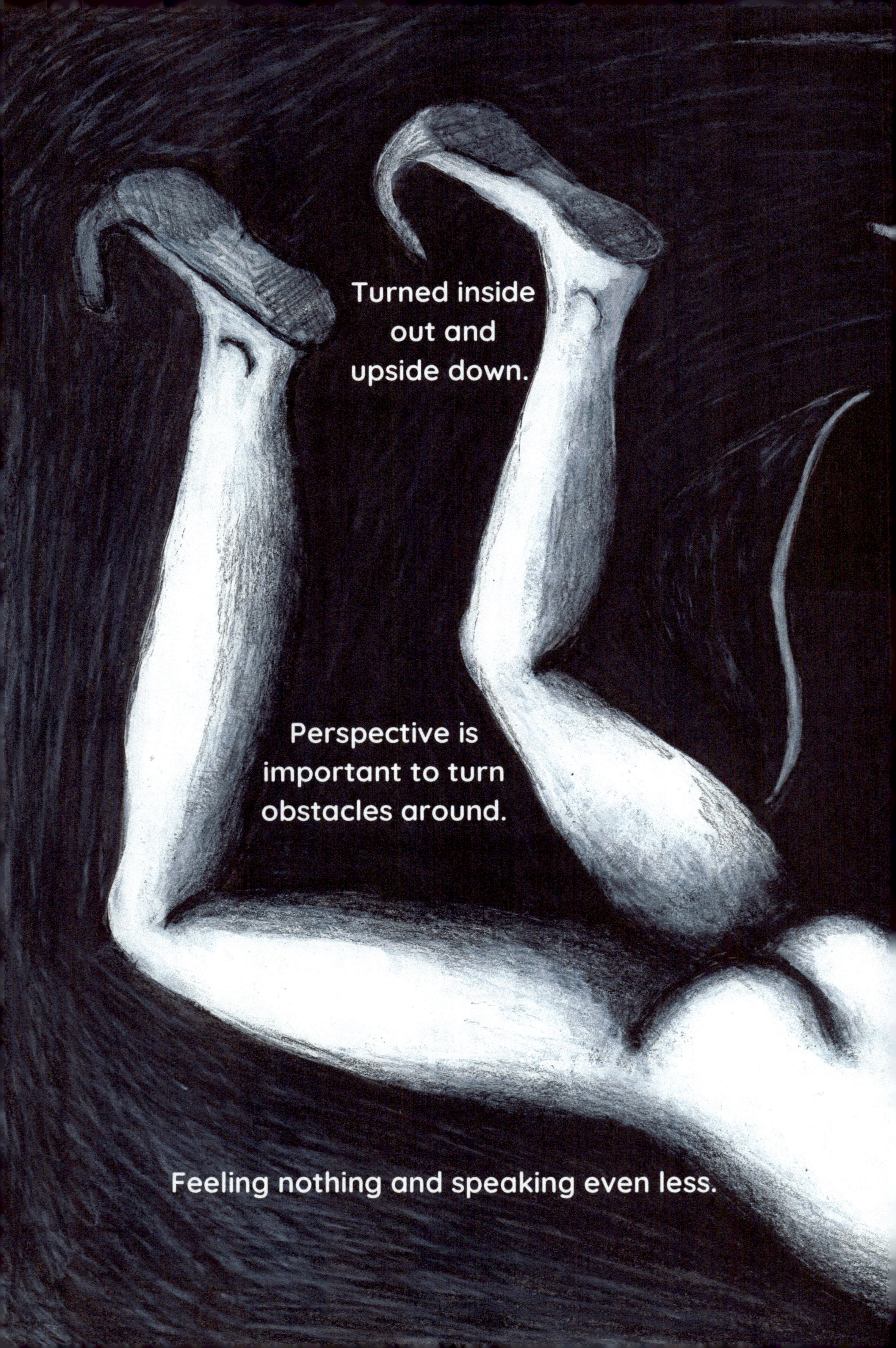

Turned inside
out and
upside down.

Perspective is
important to turn
obstacles around.

Feeling nothing and speaking even less.

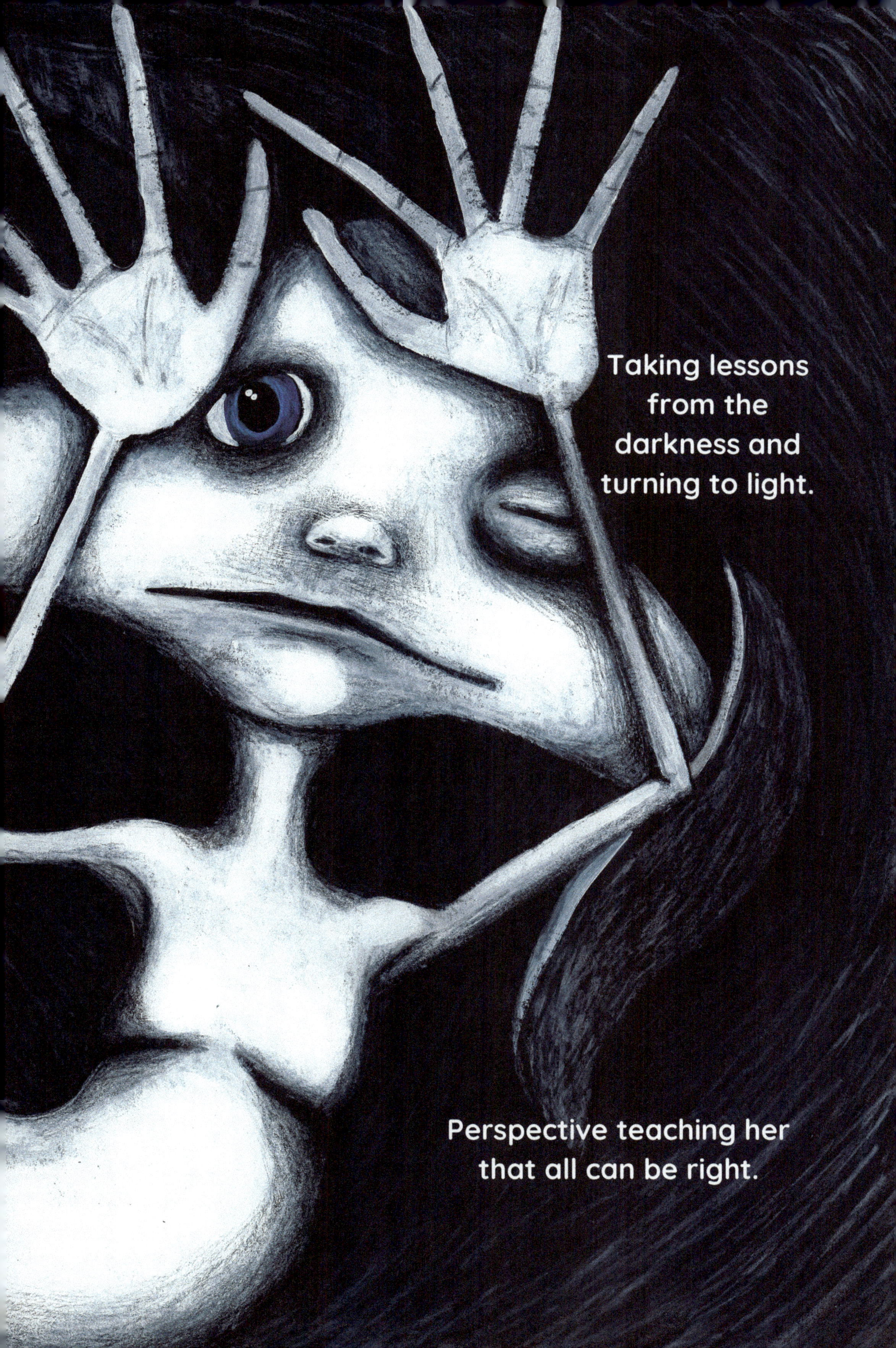

Taking lessons
from the
darkness and
turning to light.
Perspective teaching her
that all can be right.

In a silent world of painful nothingness,
she knows this is not just.

Nothingness and isolated.
To be treated fairly, is not what she got.

Tears overflowing with fear, shame and guilt.
Even in her brokenness her heart wishes to be
rebuilt.

A slight beacon of light is all she will need.
Over there, a tiny golden seed!

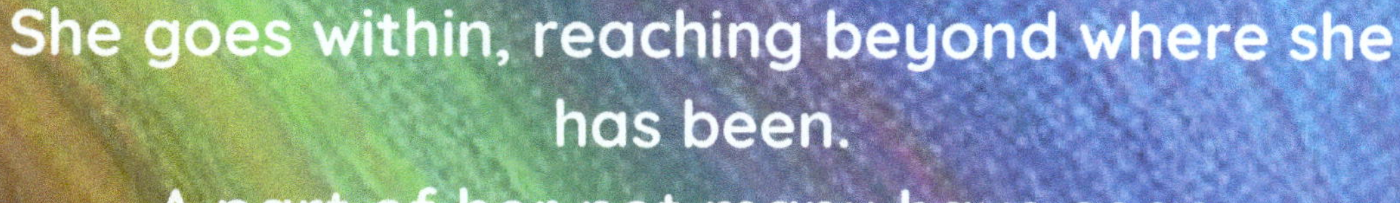

She goes within, reaching beyond where she
has been.
A part of her not many have seen.

Her trust taken, stolen and twisted, not
easily given, not even when requested.
Trusting not many, a deep knowing her heart
deserves different.

Craving connection and a sense of
belonging, surrounded by warmth, hope and
love.

Trusting her heart, there is a flicker of light.

Letting go of fear and trusting whole heartedly.
Intuition guiding, trust, hope and perseverance
forging the untrodden path.

Her out-stretched fingers cautiously and
curiously touched the tiny golden seed.
Her dreams, hopes and wishes answered.

Her wordlessness heard.
Her heart's desires fulfilled like a beautiful tune
from a darling bluebird.

Connection made, self regulation returns to
where it had once been.

Taking a breath to regulate emotions,
from ghost-like white, now back to bright green.

Holding her precious golden gift tight.
Hope restoring the feeling, the world isn't all bad.
Isolation and loneliness always in sight.
Open mindedness, she knows always steering her right.

Taking a deep breath
pushing away fear.

Learning to trust is healing her brokenness.
Her love and appreciation of beauty keeping
the tiny golden seed ever so near.

Faith brings hope and hope brings light.

A zest for life and all things good
surround her tight.

Bathed in a bright rainbow ribbon of
colour.

She feels for the first time the
possibility of a better tomorrow.

An appreciation of beauty and excellence.
Able to breathe in deeply and wholly.
Her body fills with warmth, life and deep love.

Floating into restful peace and sleep.
Knowing in her head and feeling in
her heart the darkness recede.

Spirituality within her core.
She believes in a source higher than herself,
fear and darkness vanquished and released.
She drifts into blissful sleep.

The tiny golden seed protecting her from angst.
Receiving all the love her heart deserves and needs.

Waking in the morning,
surprised and dazed.
Curiosity swirling all around.
From within the golden seed,
she sees a tiny gaze.

Two bright, new brown eyes
curiously staring back at her.

No longer alone.

Isolation and fear are forever gone.

With bravery in her heart,
nurturing and unconditional
love came with ease.

Social intelligence is knowing the right thing to do.
The innocent, vulnerable caterpillar would never
be alone, shunned or blue.

Finding purpose, belongingness and teamwork, together.
Connection to self, her outer world grew.

Nurtured, protected, connected
and unconditionally loved.

Compassion and kindness sticking
them together like glue.

Until one day, the caterpillar's
wings grew.

Both hearts filled with love, hope
and all things good.

With humble wishes given,
just as they should.

Set free to embrace her true path
with humility and grace.

With one final gentle whoosh........

She flew with strength and glee.
Love locked in their hearts.

Trust crushed fear and gave way to new life.
Unconditional love, support and guidance
was her gift from the start.

Overflowing with dynamic colour,
no room for fear.

Love locked firmly in their hearts,
keeping memories near.

Connections treasured and trust rediscovered.
Both free to follow their own path and purpose.

With the world waiting, her delicate wings flew
to the hum of the warm summer breeze.
She sprinkled vibrant colour, calm and compassion
with creativity, brilliance and ease.

Spreading colour and light where
darkness and shadows once were.
Her creativity made the world a better
place for all.

Unconditional love and honesty were
her gift to herself and the world.

Her forgiveness brought inner peace
and strength mending brokenness.
Knowing she was deserving of love and
nothing less.

Her fear, shame and guilt
transformed into this story.

She's able to share her once
unheard voice in all its glory.

Blame shifted and fear replaced,
all in the rightful place.

Standing in her strength with courage
and bravery at her core.

Empowered and visible with shadows and light aligned.
Thankful for the lessons learned.

What is next to come?